The
FRIGHT BEFORE
Christmas

HAROLD & CHESTER

IN

The

FRIGHT BEFORE

Christmas

JAMES HOWE

Illustrated by

LESLIE MORRILL

Morrow Junior Books / New York

TO AMY BERKOWER—

with thanks

Text copyright © 1988 by James Howe
Illustrations copyright © 1988 by Leslie Morrill
All rights reserved.
No part of this book may be reproduced or utilized
in any form or by any means, electronic or mechanical,
including photocopying, recording or by any information storage and retrieval system,
without permission in writing from the Publisher.
Inquiries should be addressed to
William Morrow and Company, Inc.,
105 Madison Avenue,
New York, NY 10016.

Printed in the United States of America.
1 2 3 4 5 6 7 8 9 10

Library of Congress Cataloging-in-Publication Data
Howe, James, 1946–
The fright before Christmas / by James Howe ; illustrated by
Leslie Morrill.
p.   cm.
Summary: Harold the dog and Chester the cat try to figure out why
Howie the puppy dreads the arrival of Santa Claus.
ISBN 0-688-07664-5. ISBN 0-688-07665-3 (lib. bdg.)
[1. Christmas—Fiction. 2. Fear—Fiction. 3. Santa Claus—
Fiction. 4. Animals—Fiction.] I. Morrill, Leslie H., ill.
II. Title.
PZ7.H83727Fr 1988
[E]—dc19   87-26280
CIP
AC

A Note to the Reader

It may surprise you to learn that the story you are about to read is told by a dog. But Harold is no ordinary dog. He has written other books about his family, the Monroes, and his friends: Chester, a cat; Howie, a dachshund puppy; and Bunnicula, a most unusual rabbit.

When Harold sent this story to me, he enclosed a note that read as follows:

It was Howie's first Christmas. I thought he was looking forward to it, but I found out that he was scared! Scared of Christmas? Chester had his own ideas why. And, as usual, I went along to see if he was right.

Here's the story of what happened. I hope you like it.

I did like Harold's story. And, Merry Christmas or Scary Christmas, I hope you like it, too.

—THE EDITOR

It was Christmas Eve at the Monroes' house. And Howie was scared.

"What do you mean a big fat man in a red suit is going to come down the chimney?" he said. "What does he want?"

"He doesn't *want* anything," I explained. "He has this bag he carries over his shoulder and—"

Howie ran out of the room before I could finish my sentence.

"Why do you suppose Howie is so afraid of Santa Claus?" I asked Chester.

Chester didn't answer. He was rolling around on the floor, playing cute. Chester always tries to get in a little extra cuteness the day before Christmas because he thinks he'll get more presents that way.

When I finally had his attention, his answer surprised me.

"Maybe he isn't afraid of Santa Claus, Harold," he said. "Maybe he's afraid of ghosts."

"Ghosts? This is Christmas, not Halloween."

"That may be," Chester said, "but don't you remember when Mr. Monroe read us *A Christmas Carol* by Charles Dickens? There were ghosts in that story. They walked through walls and rattled their chains. And when did they appear? On Christmas Eve! No wonder Howie's afraid."

And no wonder I had a hard time falling asleep that night. It's never easy to sleep the night before Christmas, but when you have *ghosts* to worry about, it's almost impossible!

I lay awake watching the snowflakes fall outside the kitchen window and listening to the wind stir the evergreens.

At long last, I felt my eyelids grow heavy and I drifted off.

Sometime in the middle of the night, Chester woke me. "Do you hear that?" he whispered.

"Do I hear what?"

"Those noises. There's a ghost in the house."

I stopped him before he could say anything else. I wasn't entirely convinced about this ghost business. And I didn't want Chester waking Howie up and getting him scared all over again.

But then I began to hear the noises myself. Something was moving around.

It wasn't Howie. He seemed to be sleeping soundly under the kitchen table.

"Come on," said Chester.

Upstairs, we peeked into the Monroes' bedroom. Mrs. Monroe turned in their bed. Mr. Monroe whistled through his nose. They were fast asleep.

Toby was curled up in his bed with a bear under one arm and a car under the other. "No ghosts here," I whispered to Chester.
He grunted and we went on to Pete's room.

Pete lay in the middle of his bed, his hands rolled into fists as if he were ready for a fight. Pete's that kind of kid.
But he didn't look like he'd been fighting any ghosts.

Chester and I sat at the top of the stairs for a long time, listening.
The only sound we heard was the ticking of the grandfather clock in
the hall below.

I yawned. "I think all the ghosts have gone to bed," I said.

So we headed back downstairs.

In the living room, we heard a soft rustling sound. Chester's ears perked up. Bunnicula was moving around in his cage.

"The rabbit!" Chester cried. "I should have known."

Now I think there's something I should tell you here about this rabbit of ours. He is—or so Chester says—a vampire. Don't get excited; he only attacks vegetables. Still, Chester is always ready to blame the little guy for anything strange that happens. Fortunately, before Chester had the chance this time, Bunnicula was saved by a resounding CRASH!

"The cellar!" said Chester. "We've been looking in the wrong places. In *A Christmas Carol,* one of the ghosts comes up from the cellar. Remember the rattling chains, Harold?"

The cellar was dark and full of shadows. I bumped into Chester, and we stopped in our tracks.

"What is it?" I asked.

"Straight ahead," he hissed. "Don't you see it?"

As my eyes grew used to the darkness, I saw what Chester was talking about. Could it be possible? Was it true? There, not five feet in front of us was—

THE GHOST!
Chester went wild. He jumped up.

And the ghost fell down.

"Wait! This isn't a ghost," I said. "It's only Mr. Monroe's Santa Claus costume. He must have taken it out to wear tomorrow. Say, I have an idea."

"Will your idea help us catch our ghost?" Chester asked.

"Well, no," I admitted. But I told him anyway. "I'll put this on and pretend to be Santa Claus."

Chester looked at me as if I had a screw loose.

"Don't you get it?" I said. "When Howie wakes up, he'll see a friendly Santa—his old Uncle Harold—and he won't be scared anymore."

"*If* Santa Claus is what he's scared of," said Chester.

It wasn't easy getting into the suit. I was only halfway there when I heard someone breathing. And it didn't sound like Chester.

"Do ghosts breathe?" I asked, although I wasn't sure I wanted to know the answer.

"In the corner!" Chester yelled. "Behind that pile of junk! Come out, ghost! Show yourself!"

All at once, the breathing stopped. Then something moved, and . . .

"Howie!" Chester cried. "What are you doing down here?"

Howie was shaking. "I was . . . I was trying to hide from Santa Claus," he said.

"*You* were making all the noise down here," said Chester. "We thought you were asleep in the kitchen."

"I bunched up my rug," Howie said. "I didn't want you to come looking for me. I wanted to be sure when Santa came that nobody would know where to find me."

"So you're our Christmas ghost," I said with a chuckle. I stepped into a pool of moonlight.

"Santa!" Howie yelped when he saw me. He streaked past but skidded to a halt at the bottom of the stairs.

The floorboards moved above us. They creaked. They squeaked.
And then the doorknob began to rattle.
"H-help," Howie said in a tiny voice.
"Ghosts!" Chester gulped.
My mouth fell open, but I had nothing to say.

The doorknob turned slowly. Howie ran back and forth, yipping with all his might. He ran faster and faster until he smacked right into a lamp. Down it came with a shattering crash, the shade landing on Howie's head. Chester and I cowered in a corner, hoping that the shadows would hide us. The door at the top of the stairs flew open with a bang.

From under his lampshade, Howie started to howl.

Chester hissed.

And Mrs. Monroe turned on the cellar light.

"*What* is going on down here?" she cried.

"Harold!" said Toby. "How come you're dressed up like Santa Claus?"

Toby and Pete ran down the stairs.

"Look, Mom," said Pete. "Howie broke a lamp!"

He took the shade off Howie's head and scooped him up. "That's the third time you've been bad this week," he said, wagging a finger at him. "This time the dogcatcher really will come and get you."

"The dogcatcher?" asked Toby. "What are you talking about?"

"On Monday, Howie ate the last page of my mystery book," said Pete. "And on Thursday, he broke my plastic skeleton that took me *two months* to put together. I told him if he didn't stop wrecking my stuff, the dogcatcher would come and take him away."

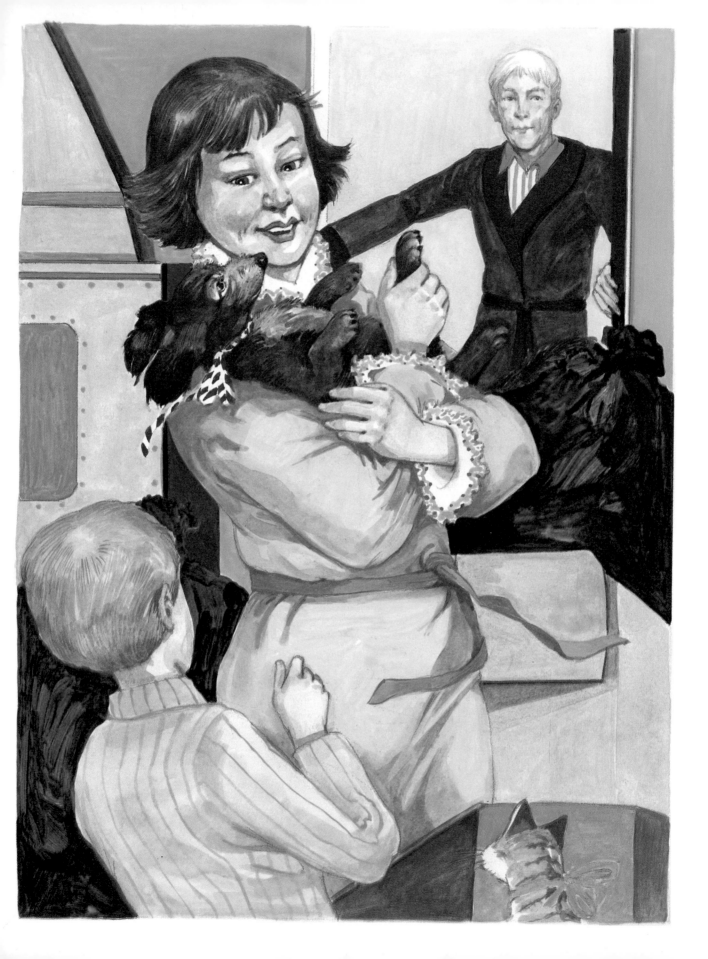

"Poor Howie," said Mrs. Monroe, taking him from Pete's arms. "No dogcatcher is going to get you. You can't help it if you break things sometimes. You're just a puppy. You still have a lot to learn."

"So this is where all the noise is coming from," Mr. Monroe said from the top of the stairs. "What do you suppose they're so excited about?"

"Christmas, I'll bet," said Toby. "Nobody can sleep the night before Christmas."

"Well, I know someone else who hasn't been sleeping," Mr. Monroe said.

Toby and Pete looked at each other and shouted, "Santa Claus!" They flew up the stairs.

Mr. and Mrs. Monroe laughed. "Well, come on, you two," Mrs. Monroe said to Chester and me.

"Shall we?" I asked Chester. "Or do you want to stay down here with the ghosts?"

"Bah, humbug," Chester muttered. But I could see by the twinkle in his eyes that all his thoughts of Christmas ghosts had passed and he was now thinking of Christmas presents instead.

"Just remember," he said as we followed the Monroes up the stairs, "*I* get to play with the ribbons."

"Did Santa Claus bring all this stuff?" Howie asked, jumping down from Mrs. Monroe's arms.

"Of course," I said. "That's what I was trying to tell you. He carries presents in his bag and leaves them under Christmas trees all over the world."

Howie shook his head. "And here I thought he used that bag to carry off bad puppies. That's what Pete said." He sighed. "At least that's what I *thought* he said. Mrs. Monroe is right, Uncle Harold. I *do* have a lot to learn."

"Merry Christmas, you guys," Toby shouted as he ran to us.

I licked his face all over. And Chester rubbed up against his legs and purred. Toby laughed and laughed. Soon the whole family was laughing.

Howie looked puzzled at first, as if he were trying to figure out what he was hearing.

Then his eyes lit up. He knew. It was the sound of Christmas. And it wasn't scary at all.